Mini
and
Hardly
and the
Big Adventure

Catherine Rayner

MACMILLAN CHILDREN'S BOOKS

Mini and Hardly are still quite little.

"It's not easy being small," huffed Mini.
"It's not easy being smaller," muttered Hardly.

They would like to be a bit more grown-up, right now.

South Dublin Libraries

www.southdublinlibraries.ie

"If we were older we could eat
anything we fancied!" Mini marvelled.
"Whenever we wanted!"

"If we were a bit bigger, we'd be able
to gallop much faster," said Hardly.
"And also, big unicorns can neigh really loudly."

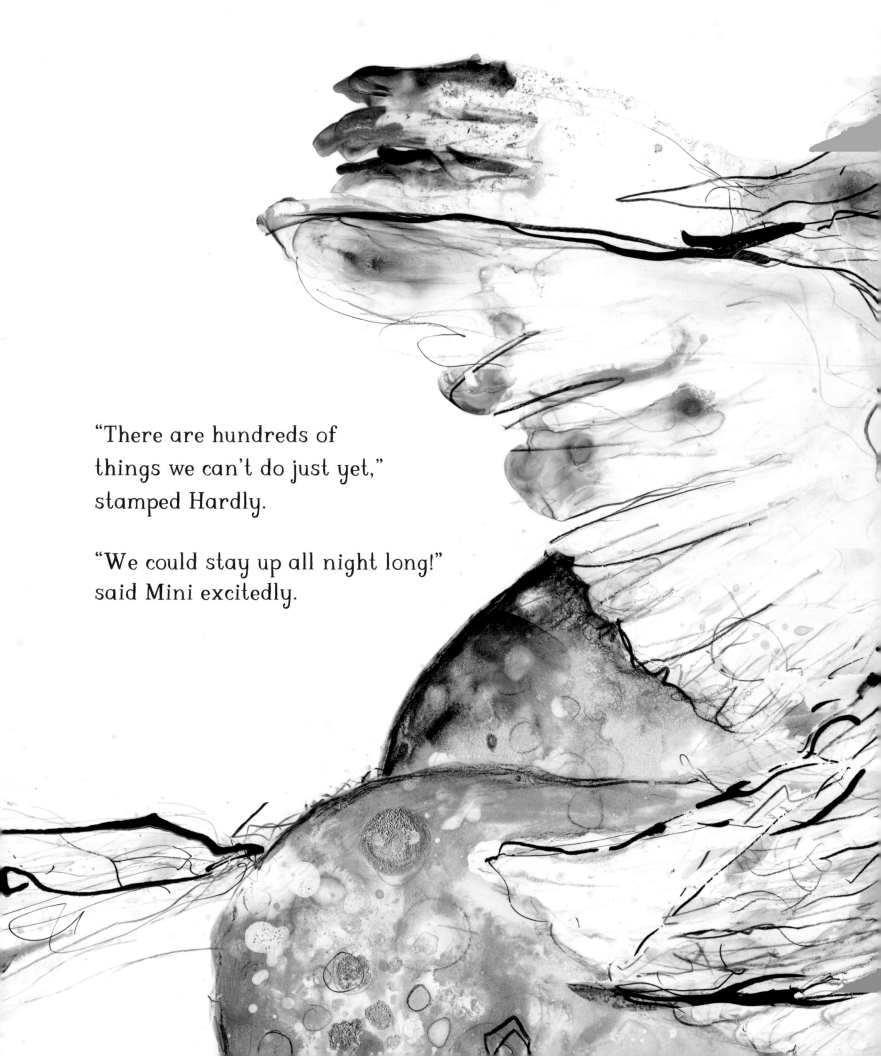

"There are hundreds of things we can't do just yet," stamped Hardly.

"We could stay up all night long!" said Mini excitedly.

"We could play games until dawn," Hardly squealed.
"Or go on a big adventure!"

Mini kicked his heels in the air and
they both bounced with excitement.

"Let's not wait! Let's go on that big adventure
RIGHT NOW!" squealed Hardly . . .

So off they went.

They trotted up hills and they cantered through cactus fields.

They raced between mountains
and flew over huge forests.

They felt very big and very grown-up
and **VERY** important.

Until . . .

"Where are we?" said Mini.
"I don't know," answered Hardly, looking around,
"but the sky is getting dark."

"The waves are wild," trembled Mini,
in a tiny voice. "I hope there won't be thunder."

"I'm cold," Hardly started to shiver.

Mini and Hardly didn't feel
quite so big anymore.

Crash went the waves . . .

and **howl** went the wind.

The little unicorns tried not to cry.

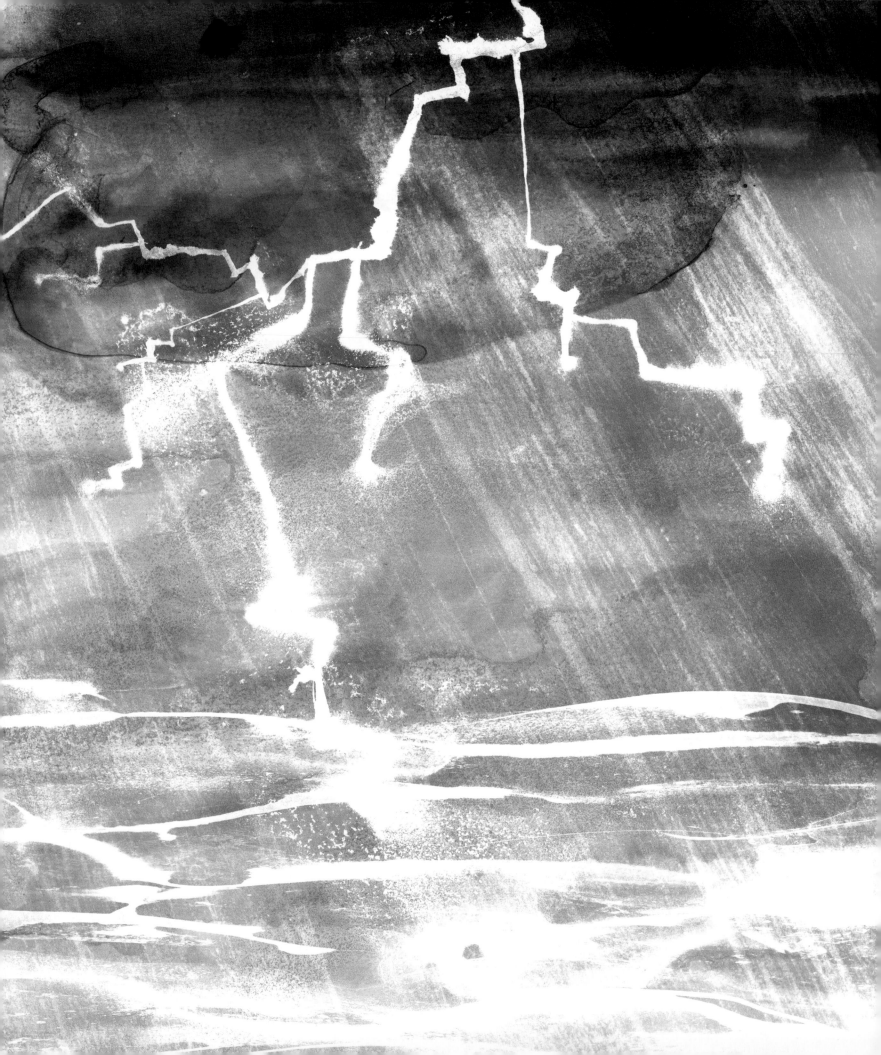

Then, in between rumbles and crashes,
they heard another noise in the distance.

It sounded like the beating of wings.

"There you are little ones! I was wondering where you'd gone! Come now, it's getting late and it's time to go home."

Mini and Hardly walked along,
thinking quietly for a while.

"It's actually quite nice feeling little,"
said Hardly at last.

"Yes it is," Mini agreed.
"And it's quite nice being looked
after. We'll be big soon enough!"

"Actually," Mini whinnied, "I think we are fine just the way we are, right now!"

"Yes, we are. Right now we are perfect!" laughed Hardly. "And I'm not sure we are ready for BIG adventures just yet."

"So, shall we just practise being big at home?" Hardly asked.

"That's a good idea," chuckled Mini. "Let's grow up later on!"

"Because after all," whispered Hardly, "being small makes you perfect for the biggest of cuddles."

"Yes," said Mini, "it's lovely being small."

"Come to think of it," said Hardly, "it's even better being smaller!"

For Florence and Emily, and all the
big adventures they will have.

xxx

First published 2021 by Macmillan Children's Books
This edition published 2022 by Macmillan Children's Books
an imprint of Pan Macmillan
The Smithson, 6 Briset Street, London EC1M 5NR
EU representative: Macmillan Publishers Ireland Ltd, 1st Floor,
The Liffey Trust Centre, 117–126 Sheriff Street Upper,
Dublin 1, D01 YC43
Associated companies throughout the world.
www.panmacmillan.com

ISBN: 978-1-5098-0423-8

Text and Illustrations copyright © Catherine Rayner 2021

The right of Catherine Rayner to be identified as the author and illustrator of this work
has been asserted by her in accordance with the Copyright, Designs and Patents Act 1988.

All rights reserved. No part of this publication may be reproduced, stored in a retrieval system,
or transmitted, in any form or by any means (electronic, mechanical, photocopying,
recording or otherwise), without the prior written permission of the publisher.

1 3 5 7 9 8 6 4 2

A CIP catalogue record for this book is available from the British Library.

Printed in China.

FSC
www.fsc.org

MIX
Paper from
responsible sources
FSC® C116313